3

One day, something crawled
up Big's leg,
up Big's tail,
and up Big's back.
It was a little angry mouse.

"Oh you monster!" cried the mouse.
"You stomped over my garden!"

"Sorry," said Big. "I'm very sorry."

Le   ds

Big the elephant was lonely.
He was the biggest animal
in the forest and didn't have a friend.

When Big was lonely and bored,
he would stomp up and down.
Stomp! Stomp! Stomp!
That made him feel better.

5

"My name is Big," said the elephant.
"I'm the biggest animal in the forest."

"My name is Little," said the mouse.
"I'm the littlest animal in the forest.
Why do you stomp around like that?"

"I'm lonely," said Big. "I'm big and slow
and nobody wants to play with me."

"Really?" said Little.
"No one plays with me
because they say I'm too little."

At that moment,
a great idea came to Big and Little.
"Let's be friends!" they said together.

Big was so excited, he stomped
and stomped and stomped.
Little hung on to Big's tail
and swung and swung and swung.
"YIPPEE!" they shouted.

9

Every day,
Big and Little played together.
They ate together.
They sang songs together.

They gave each other gifts.

They gave each other letters.

Big and Little were the best of friends.

As Big and Little grew closer,
someone became upset.
It was Moley the mole
who lived underground.

Little came running by
with an acorn pie and a letter
to give to his friend Big.

Moley stopped him.
"Hey, Little! Come here!
I have something to tell you!"

Then Moley whispered
in Little's ear.

Soon after, Big came along.

"Hi, Little!" he said with a smile.

But Little was not happy to see Big.

He said, "You think I'm too little!

My writing is so small you can't read it!

My acorn pie is so small you can't taste it!

How can you say that about me?

I thought you were my friend!"

Then Little scurried away.

15

Big sat down under a tree.
Moley came up to him.
"Hey, slowpoke!" said Moley.
"Little says you are so slow,
you make him want to pull
his whiskers out.
He says you stomp so hard,
you give him a headache."

Big's heart began to ache.
"Little said that about me?"

Slowly, Big walked away.
His eyes watered as he thought
of all the good times
he and Little had shared.

Just then, in the grass,
he heard a sobbing sound.

Little was crying. He said,

"Big, I don't care if you said I'm too small.

Let's still be friends."

"But Little," Big replied,

"I never said anything like that.

It was you who said I was slow."

"What?" cried Little. "I never did!"

They were speechless for a moment.

Then they cried out together,

"MOLEY!"

21

"Moley!" they said.
"Why did you do that to us?"

Tears fell from Moley's eyes.
"I'm sorry. I was jealous.
You are such good friends.
No one wants to play with me
because I can't see well."

"Oh Moley!" cried Big and Little.

"Let's all be friends!"

25

Hi Guys,

It's me, Moley.
Big, when I first saw you,
I was surprised. You are heavy
but you can run really fast.
Little, your stories are fun.
They make me laugh and laugh.
When I saw that you were
friends, I felt lonely and jealous.
I felt I was the only one
who didn't have a friend.
I am so sorry for what I did.
Thank you for understanding
what I was feeling.
You two have taught me
what friendship is all about.
These days, I'm very happy.

Your friend,
Moley

big & SMALL

Original Korean text by Seo-yun Choi
Illustrations by Masumi Furukawa
Original Korean edition © Eenbook

This English edition published by big & SMALL
by arrangement with Eenbook
English text edited by Joy Cowley
Additional editing by Mary Lindeen
Artwork for this edition produced
in cooperation with Norwood House Press, U.S.A.
English edition © big & SMALL 2015

ISBN: 978-1-925233-92-6

Printed in Korea